W9-AXE-047

Mighty Machines

Jets

by Matt Doeden

Consulting Editor: Gail Saunders-Smith, PhD

Consultant: Nathan W. McKelvey
President and Founder of jets.com
Member of the National Business Aviation Association

Capstone
press

Mankato, Minnesota

Pebble Plus is published by Capstone Press,
151 Good Counsel Drive, P.O. Box 669, Mankato, Minnesota 56002.
www.capstonepub.com

Books published by Capstone Press are manufactured with paper
containing at least 10 percent post-consumer waste.

Library of Congress Cataloging-in-Publication Data
Doeden, Matt.
    Jets / by Matt Doeden.
        p. cm.—(Pebble Plus: Mighty machines)
    Summary: "Simple text and photographs describe jets, their parts, and what they do"
—Provided by publisher.
    Includes bibliographical references and index.
    ISBN-13: 978-0-7368-6719-1 (hardcover)
    ISBN-10: 0-7368-6719-8 (hardcover)
1. Jet planes—Juvenile literature. I. Title. II. Series: Pebble plus. Mighty machines.
TL709.D55 2006
629.133'349—dc22   2006014715

Editorial Credits
Mari Schuh, editor; Molly Nei, set designer; Patrick D. Dentinger, book designer; Jo Miller,
        photo researcher/photo editor

Photo Credits
Check Six/George Hall, cover, 14–15
Corbis/zefa/Wolfgang, 12–13
David R. Frazier Photolibrary Inc., 8–9
Getty Images Inc./The Image Bank/Lester Lefkowitz, 20–21
Index Stock Imagery/Greg Kiger, 10–11
Photo by Ted Carolson/Fotodynamics, 4–5, 18–19
Shutterstock/vm, 1
Unicorn Stock Photos/Paul A. Hein, 6–7; Steve Bourgeois, 16–17

Note to Parents and Teachers

The Mighty Machines set supports national social studies standards related to science, technology, and society. This book describes and illustrates jets. The images support early readers in understanding the text. The repetition of words and phrases helps early readers learn new words. This book also introduces early readers to subject-specific vocabulary words, which are defined in the Glossary section. Early readers may need assistance to read some words and to use the Table of Contents, Glossary, Read More, Internet Sites, and Index sections of the book.

Printed in the United States of America in North Mankato, Minnesota.
012011
006069R

Table of Contents

Jets

Jets fly very high

in the sky.

Jets are fast airplanes.

Parts of Jets

Jet engines give jets speed.

Engines roar.

Jets take off from runways.

engine

Long wings lift jets
into the air.
Wing flaps help jets
take off and land.

wing flap

Pilots fly jets
from inside cockpits.
The cockpit has
many controls.

Wheels tuck up
inside jets while they fly.

Jet wheels come down.

Then jets safely land.

Kinds of Jets

Passenger jets carry people
from one airport to another.

Military jets
fight in battles.

Mighty Machines

Jets zoom across the sky.

Jets are mighty machines.

Glossary

battle—a fight between two military groups

cockpit—the room where a pilot sits in a plane

jet engine—an engine that uses streams of hot gas to make power

military—the armed forces of a country

pilot—a person who flies a jet or plane

runway—a long, flat piece of ground where a jet can take off or land

Read More

Braulick, Carrie A. *Jets.* Blazers: Horsepower. Mankato, Minn.: Capstone Press, 2007.

Doeden, Matt. *Fighter Planes.* Mighty Machines. Mankato, Minn.: Capstone Press, 2004.

Hill, Lee Sullivan. *Jets.* Pull Ahead Books. Minneapolis: Lerner, 2005.

Internet Sites

FactHound offers a safe, fun way to find Internet sites related to this book. All of the sites on FactHound have been researched by our staff.

Here's how:

1. Visit *www.facthound.com*

2. Choose your grade level.

3. Type in this book ID **0736867198** for age-appropriate sites. You may also browse subjects by clicking on letters, or by clicking on pictures and words.

4. Click on the **Fetch It** button.

FactHound will fetch the best sites for you!

Index

Word Count: 88
Grade: 1
Early-Intervention Level: 13